This board book belongs to

_____

_____

_____

For my pesky little sisters,
Becky and Jess, with love.

ORCHARD BOOKS

First published in Great Britain in 2007 by Orchard Books
This edition published in 2020 by The Watts Publishing Group

1 3 5 7 9 10 8 6 4 2

Text and illustrations © Sam Lloyd, 2007

The moral rights of the author-illustrator have been asserted.

A CIP catalogue record for this book is available from the British Library.

ISBN 978 1 40836 072 9

Printed and bound in China

MIX
Paper from
responsible sources
FSC® C104740
FSC
www.fsc.org

Orchard Books
An imprint of Hachette Children's Group
Part of The Watts Publishing Group Limited
Carmelite House
50 Victoria Embankment
London EC4Y 0DZ

An Hachette UK Company
www.hachette.co.uk

www.hachettechildrens.co.uk

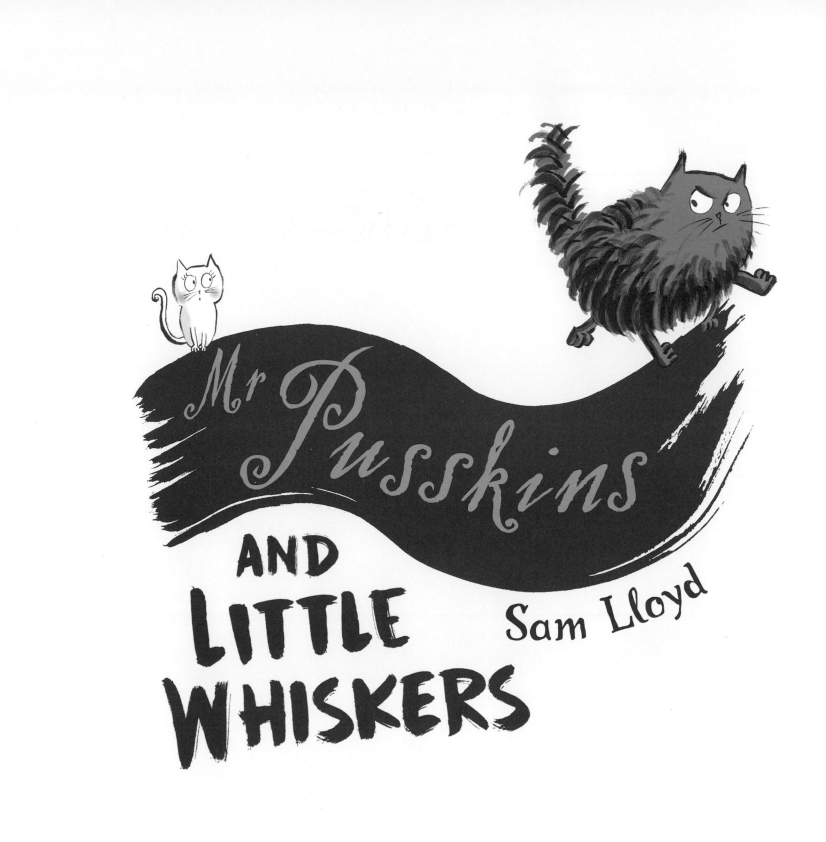

Mr Pusskins
AND LITTLE WHISKERS

Sam Lloyd

ORCHARD

This is the story of a little girl called Emily, and her dear cat, Mr Pusskins.

Dum diddley dum dum, doo doo doo,
Sharing magic moments, just us two.

Love songs

They thought life couldn't get any better.

Then, one day, Emily announced that she had a fabulous surprise for Mr Pusskins. He was **very** excited.

Emily fetched a large cardboard box, and inside the box was ...

"This is Little Whiskers," said Emily. "She has come to live with us. She is only a tiny kitten, so we need to take care of her."

"I'm sure you two will be the best of friends," smiled Emily, "so I'll leave you to play lovely games together."

Mr Pusskins needed to be alone.
He was somewhat disappointed with his
'fabulous surprise', and he certainly
wasn't in the mood for 'lovely games'.

Little Whiskers wasn't in the mood
for **lovely games** either . . .

The pesky kitten took great delight in ruining all Mr Pusskins' special times.

She ruined telly time...

she ruined meal time...

she ruined play time...

she ruined nap time . . .

When Emily wasn't looking, Little Whiskers ruined

EVERYTHING!

Mr Pusskins could bear it no longer.
Something had to be done.

So, that evening, Mr Pusskins wrote a letter.

To whom it may concern,
I am displeased with my 'fabulous surprise'. I find the kitten EXTREMELY irritating and wish to return her ASAP.
Yours fed-up-ingly,
Mr P

Tomorrow he would send it!

Then, Mr Pusskins
settled down for
a nice long sleep . . .

BAM
BAM

Suddenly, a hideous
noise woke him.
He dashed to
see what was
going on . . .

CLUNK CLUNK

Emily dashed too. And who did she see?
"Mr Pusskins!" she gasped. "You know better
than to play such a terrible tune at this time
of night. You might have woken Little Whiskers!"

Emily banished Mr Pusskins outside.
"You need to think about what you've
done wrong," she said.

But Mr Pusskins hadn't done anything wrong. As rain turned to snow, he thought about his cosy home.

He reached up to the window to take
a peek . . . That wretched kitten! She was
already sitting in Mr Pusskins' favourite
spot by the fireside. Mr Pusskins was

FURIOUS!

But Little Whiskers wasn't enjoying the fireside. She knew **she** had been behaving naughtily, **not** Mr Pusskins.

How she wished there was a way she could make things better. And there was ...

Little Whiskers leapt onto the piano . . .

BAM BAM
CLUNK CLUNK
BOOM BOOM BOOM

In rushed Emily. "Oh, good gracious!" she gasped. "Little Whiskers! It was **you** that played that terrible tune, wasn't it?!"

"Miaow," admitted the kitten.

Emily hurried outside. "My poor Mr Pusskins!
Please forgive me," she begged.
And, of course, Mr Pusskins did.

Little Whiskers
asked Mr Pusskins
to forgive her too.

And, eventually...

Mr Pusskins
DID!

Mr Pusskins didn't send the letter after all. He decided Little Whiskers could stay.

This is the end of the story of a little girl called Emily, and her dear cats, Mr Pusskins and Little Whiskers.